I

Maddie Wants Music

Illustrations Marie-Louise Gay

Translation by Sarah Cummins

Formac Publishing Company Limited
Halifax, Nova Scotia 1993

Katie Ark.

Canadian Cataloguing in Publication Data

Leblanc, Louise, 1942-

[Ça va mal pour Sophie. English]

Maddie wants music

(First Novel Series)

Translation of: Ça va mal pour Sophie.
ISBN 0-88780-219-2 (pbk.) — ISBN 0-88780-220-6 (bound)

I. Gay, Marie-Louise. II. Title. III. Title Ça va mal pour Sophie. English. IV. Series.

PS8573.D25C3413 1992   jC843'.54   C92-098740-0
PZ7.L42Mad 1992

Formac Publishing Company Limited
5502 Atlantic Street
Halifax N.S. B3H 1G4

Printed and bound in Canada

Table of Contents

1
I hate opera!

It's spring! The sky is blue, birds are singing in the trees, and everyone is happy. Everyone except me.

That's the way it was the day I wanted to listen to some music, but couldn't. That's nothing new. I can never do what I want.

In the living room my parents were listening to opera. Opera is a kind of music that goes on and on. It sounds like gulls screeching and witches cackling.

My little sister, Angelbaby Sugarkins, was having her nap.

I don't know how she could sleep through all that racket.

I went down to the basement, and found my brother Julian watching *The Moontrippers* for the one hundredth time.

My brother Alexander was playing monster battle. Whenever the monster army attacked he let out strange and horrible screams.

I hurried back upstairs. I announced to my parents that I had found a solution to my problem.

At that very moment one of the opera singers began to laugh her bloodcurdling laugh. I was sure my parents hadn't heard a word I said. So I yelled, "IF I HAD A WALKMAN, I COULD LISTEN TO SOME MUSIC!"

I guess it wasn't my lucky day, because at that very instant the singer stopped.

"I think you might find a better way to ask," my father remarked.

However, he did inquire, "How much does a walkman cost?"

"Only fifty dollars!"

"FIFTY DOLLARS?" my mother echoed.

"You can start by saving some money," said my father, "and then we'll discuss it."

My mother liked that idea.

"We could give you a quarter for every time you..."

As she listed every little chore I could do, all the opera singers began to shriek at once. There was a tremendous crashing of cymbals and drums.

Angelbaby woke up and began

to cry.

In my opinion, it was too noisy to add up quarters, so I went outside.

I got the feeling my parents were not pleased with me. And to make matters worse, they said that I woke up Angelbaby.

UNBELIEVABLE!

2
Trouble in the tree

In any case, I'm going to get started on my plan to get a Zesty walkman. I've got to have one. That's all there is to it.

When I saw the ad in the newspaper, it was love at first sight. The Zesty looks like a big lemon drop. It's probably called Zesty because lemons put zest into cooking.

It must be a very good walkman. It said in big yellow letters in the newspaper:

"MAGICAL SOUND!

"JUST TURN ON YOUR ZESTY AND YOUR FAVOURITE

SINGER IS RIGHT THERE
WITH YOU!"

Can you believe it!?

I would love to have Bryan
Adams right there with me. Wow!

But I wanted to think it over. I
wasn't sure my parents' plan
was a good one.

I decided to go climb the tree
that stands between our back
yard and our next door
neighbours'. Nobody had lived
in that house for more than a
year, so I could count on a bit of
privacy.

My father says the tree is
extraordinary. That means it's
unusual. I think it's wonderful.
It has nine separate branches
growing out in different directions.

I pushed through the lowest
branches down near the ground

and settled into the middle where a carpet of moss grew, softer even than our living room rug. And I began to think.

1. The Zesty walkman costs $50. That is VERY expensive, although of course I didn't say so to my parents.

2. I only have $11.38 in my piggy bank. Not very much.

3. The difference between $50 and $11.38 is exactly ... um ... well, it comes to around $40. Yikes!

4. I think I will refuse my parents' offer. If I earn money by doing chores for them, I won't be able to buy my Zesty until I'm 95 years old.

Do you realize how many chores I would have to do at 25 cents each before I earned $40?

I don't even want to think about it.

5. I can't work anywhere else. My parents would never let me, that's for sure. And anyway, there's already too much unemployment.

Since there's no way I can earn the money, maybe I could borrow it! That's a good plan. I'll borrow the money. Easy as pie. Now who can I borrow it from?

OUCH! Something just landed on my head!? Yikes, was it an egg dropped by one of the birds that live up in the tree? Or a bird going to the bathroom? No, there was nothing in my hair. Whew!

I pushed aside the branches and looked up … I couldn't

believe my eyes!

Do you know who was perched on one of the branches of my tree?

A little girl … a strange little girl. She had straight black hair, falling like a mop over her head. She looked like a real punk!

Grrr! I came here for some privacy!

"Maddie! Maddie! It's dinner-time!"

For once, I was glad to hear my mom calling me. I jumped down from the tree and ran home.

What a day! Things were definitely not going smoothly.

3
Lost my appetite

"You don't look very well, Maddie."

That's what my mom told me the minute I walked into the kitchen. As usual, my dad gave me no time to explain.

"If it's because of the walkman, I don't want to hear about it now. Meal times should be a haven of calmness."

I kept very calm, and merely replied, "The walkman? I've got other problems."

But inside I didn't feel calm. Inside I was reciting what I would say to my parents if I were to tell them what I was thinking.

It's easy to be calm when you have piles of money and you can buy whatever you want, without asking permission.

"What's a walkman?" asked Julian.

I had no trouble telling Julian exactly what I was thinking.

"A walkman is a machine for listening to music even while you are watching *The Moontrippers*."

"Why would I want to listen to music while I'm watching *The Moontrippers*?"

Why bother answering? It's too depressing. Nobody ever understands anything in this house. And the worst of it is, none of them even realize it.

Julian kept munching on a celery stick and looking at me like I was crazy.

Alexander chewed on an olive and snickered. When he finished, he spat the olive pit at my eye.

It didn't hit my eye because I leaned over. It whizzed past me and landed near my mother's foot.

My mother stepped on it. But she didn't fall. All she did was drop a jar of mustard she was carrying.

Mustard went everywhere. Lots of it went into Angelbaby's mashed carrots.

Angelbaby ate an enormous spoonful of it. She choked and spat it all out.

There was carrot and mustard all over everything, especially on my father's shirt. He started to sputter.

I felt like telling him that meal times should be a haven of calmness. Instead I just said to my mother, "I'm not very hungry anymore."

It really wasn't my lucky day. The very instant I spoke, my mother placed in front of me a

triple-decker hamburger and a mountain of French fries.

"FRENCH FRIES! YIPPEE! SUPER! MY FAVOURITE!"

Well no, that's not what I said. Like an idiot, I just repeated, "I'm really not very hungry."

At last my mother began to get worried.

"If you're not hungry for French fries, something must be wrong. What is it?"

Since at last someone was interested in me, I told her about the strange little girl in my tree. I tried to eat as many French fries as I could without anyone noticing.

Do you know how to do that? First, you can't make any holes in the pile. That's no problem. You just have to push the fries back into a pile every time you take one away.

Then you must not show that you are enjoying the crispy golden French fries. That's much harder, because you still have to look like you're in a bad mood.

I think I managed pretty well, because my father said, "I hope you're not going to keep on sulking until the neighbours move away. They just got here!"

Then he laughed as if he had just said something very witty.

"I'm sure there is room for two little girls in that big tree, right? Who knows, maybe you'll make friends with her."

I ate two or three fries, looking as furious as I could.

"I doubt it. I told you, she's weird."

"I don't think you're weird. And I'm not weird either," said Julian.

As usual, he was totally tuned out.

"What do you mean?" asked my mother.

"Well, Maddie and I have straight black hair too, just like punker mopheads."

Everyone laughed, especially Alexander. He thinks he's so handsome with his blonde curls. But when he stopped laughing, it went from bad to worse. Do you know what he said?

"I think I'll buy a walkman for myself. I have lots of money in my piggy bank."

That really got me mad. If I had been any madder, I would have bitten someone. Instead, I bit into a French fry and told my parents that I really wasn't hungry at all. I said I wanted to go up to my room and think.

My parents couldn't believe it.

Alexander grabbed my hamburger. He always has to take my things and copy whatever I do.

But at least he won't get my French fries, because I ate them all.

4
Time for action

As I climbed the stairs only one thing was going through my head: Alexander was going to get a walkman, and I wasn't.

It couldn't be. It would be TOO unfair. He doesn't need a walkman to play war games. If *I* had a walkman, it would change my whole life.

When I reached the second floor, I told myself there was no more time for thinking. It was clear what I had to do.

I went into Alexander's room. It's strange, because I really don't know why I did.

The floorboards shrieked to the whole family: CREEEAK! MADDIE'S GOING INTO ALEXANDER'S ROOM! CREEAK!

The creaking stopped when I stopped at Alexander's desk, just in front of his piggy bank. All of a sudden I realized why I had come into his room.

I had come to see whether Alexander really had enough money to buy a Zesty walkman.

I stepped forward and picked up the piggy bank.

CREEAK!

I walked over to Alexander's bed.

CREAK! CREAK! CRACK!

I sat down on the bed.

ZWIINGGGG!

Now it was the bedsprings. Grrr! I never noticed before what tattletales these things are.

I felt sick. A wave of fever swept up to my head all at once. It was terrible! I felt like a thermometer about to explode.

Quick! I pulled the stopper out of the piggy bank and turned it over. Nothing happened. It was so full, the opening was blocked. With trembling hands, I shook the bank.

Finally coins began to fall on the bedspread. Millions of them! I couldn't believe how rich Alexander was! It was awful!

I could never count all that money in five minutes. That's how long it takes for Alexander to eat a hamburger.

When I remembered that there was sugar pie for dessert, I decided to separate the pennies from the other coins. Alexander always takes two helpings of sugar pie.

I put the pennies back in the piggy bank without counting them. There were too many of them and they're practically worthless.

So Alexander wasn't as rich as I had thought. That was good news.

In fact, it got better. Alexander only had $13.90. Whew! I had never added so fast in my life. I was beginning to realize that math is a VERY important subject.

I figured I had better put the piggy bank back. When I stood up, I got the shock of my life!

A ten-dollar bill dropped off my lap! I unfolded it to make sure it was real. I almost fainted.

There were two ten-dollar bills
… no, three … four.

THAT MAKES FORTY
DOLLARS!

Alexander is a millionaire! He
could buy a walkman! NO! He
can't. *I'm* going to buy a walkman, not him. Yikes! I heard a
noise.

Was I ever hot! I couldn't
stuff the ten-dollar bills back
into Alexander's piggy bank. It
was already too full. My heart
was banging inside me like an
animal caught in a trap.

Quick! I had to do something!
Put my plan into action! Right!
I'll borrow some money from
Alexander — twenty dollars.
There was just enough room to
stuff two ten-dollar bills back
into the bank.

Quick! I put the bank back on the desk and went out the door.

CREEAK!   MADDIE'S LEAVING   ALEXANDER'S ROOM! CREEAK!

I was sweating. My hair was so damp I felt like a … mophead.

5
I'm afraid!

I went back downstairs as if nothing had happened. My heart was still thumping to be let out. But nobody could hear it.

"Get your tomatoes! Lovely red tomatoes for sale!"

Alexander suspected nothing. He was playing store with Julian and Angelbaby.

What an idiotic game. They pretend to buy a bunch of non-existent things with invisible money.

Luckily, Alexander was playing storekeeper.

"Beautiful big red tomatoes!"

"'Mato?" asked Angelbaby.

"Look at the beautiful big red tomato coming down the stairs, Angelbaby!"

A big red tomato coming down the stairs. How idiotic can you get? A tomato coming down the stairs. He meant me!

Just because I borrowed some money from Alexander doesn't mean he can insult me. Anyway, what's he talking about?

"What are you talking about?"

"You. You're red as a tomato."

"I am not in the least red!"

"Yes, you are. Look in the mirror. If you were any redder, you'd be bleeding."

"Well, I'd rather look like a tomato than a cucumber."

"Not me. Cucumbers are stronger. I'm going to crush you."

"Just see if you can, cukehead!"

Alexander and I started fighting. Angelbaby was worried about me.

"Po' 'mato!"

Julian leapt in. "Desist, you saucy varlets!"

He thought he was in the middle of adventure story.

"Unhand him, or I will smite you with my invincible sword. Stop, or I will arrest you in the name of the law!"

Alexander and I couldn't care less what he did. We kept on fighting. I have never hated Alexander so much in my whole life. I think I was mad at him because I took the money from his piggy bank.

Julian was as good as his word. He leapt upon us with his

invincible sword, holding on to his glasses and yelling, "On your knees! Lay down your cudgels, uncouth knaves!"

He got a punch in the nose for his trouble and lost his glasses. Blood poured from his nose just like in the cartoons. That was when my parents walked in.

"THAT'S ENOUGH!" was all my father said.

Alexander and I immediately stopped fighting. But it was too late. Julian's glasses were broken in half and the lenses were shattered into little pieces.

My parents claimed that I had not thought about what I was doing. They suggested I go to my room to start thinking, now. They advised Alexander to do the same.

That worried me. He was all alone in his room.

I stole over to the door and

listened. I couldn't hear a thing. No pennies clinking together. It's funny, but the silence didn't make me feel any better.

I was beginning to feel hot again. I felt worse than I had when I took the money out of his piggy bank. I was beginning to feel … afraid.

It was terrible. I felt as if this whole thing would never end!

6
Lawn sale

A lot has changed in the last week. My parents finally realized that I need a walkman. They hope that peace will descend once more upon our house.

They came up with another plan for me to make money. It's better than the first one. They have suggested I hold a lawn sale.

The only problem is, they refused to give me any of their things to sell. They told me I had to sell my own things.

I started by putting aside all the toys I absolutely had to keep.

What was left was a few broken marbles, a bald doll, a bunch of stickers that wouldn't stick anymore ...

I know people will buy anything, but still, I didn't think this stuff would sell. So I decided to make some paintings, because I am a very good artist.

In a week I made about thirty paintings. I could have done a lot more if I hadn't had to keep an eye on Alexander. It made me nervous when I couldn't see what he was up to.

Alexander couldn't get over how I kept wanting to play with him. He couldn't believe I said I'd play monster in the monster war against Alexander the Terrible.

And he fell down in astonishment when I suggested we play store with Julian and Angelbaby. His eyes were as big and round as quarters.

By playing store I became an excellent saleswoman. I knew that I would be able to sell all the things in my lawn sale.

No doubt about it!

And soon, soon I would have my very own Zesty!

To open my sale at ten o'clock, I had to get all my stuff down to the sidewalk.

When I got outside, I discovered that my parents had set up a table for me. They had even put some of their own stuff on it. There's a great selection!

And Gran came! She said she was in the mood to do some shopping. My parents bought a lot of stuff too. So did Julian, and even Angelbaby. With my parents' money.

Everybody came ... except Alexander.

Inside I was panicking. "Uh-oh. What's Alexander up to?"

But I pretended to be calm and simply asked, "Where's Alexander?"

Gran tried to cheer me up. "I'm sure Alexander will come soon to buy something from you, honey."

Poor Gran, THAT was exactly what I was worried about. If only some passersby would pass by. But there was nobody. I looked to the left. Nothing. Not even a couple of little black dots that could grow and grow and turn into customers. I looked to the right. WHAT?! OH NO!

Do you know what I saw?

Our new neighbour, the one who was perched on the branch of my tree.

And do you know what she was doing?

She was holding a sale too. And her parents were helping her too, just like mine. Grrr! I can't stand copycats!

Probably she wanted to buy a walkman too. Probably she made some paintings to sell!

Uh-oh. She hadn't made paintings ... she made cakes!

Cakes! Now that's a good idea!

Things were looking bad.

7
The old babies

A lot of customers came by in the last hour. They walked right past my table and stopped at the neighbour's.

It was depressing. People just don't appreciate art. They would rather have food.

I'd have to be a better sales-person, that's all.

A bunch of little black dots were coming closer. To bolster my courage I shut my eyes. Then I yelled, "PAINTINGS FOR SALE! BEAUTIFUL PAINTINGS FOR SALE! NECKTIES! DOLLS! KNIVES

AND FORKS!"

"Hey you! You, pipsqueak!"

Wouldn't you know it. The customers passed by and went straight to the neighbour's.

I opened my eyes. Then I realized that I was the pipsqueak they were talking to.

Standing in front of my table were seven big guys all dressed alike. They were all wearing black jeans, hightop boots with metal toes, and little tee shirts stretched tight over their big muscles. And not a one had a single hair on his head.

It was unbelievable. They were all as bald as my doll. They looked really ugly, like old babies.

Even so, maybe they wanted to buy something.

"Hey, Pipsqueak here has some nice knives, doesn't she, Adolf?"

"Very nice knives, Tom."

They all seemed to think my knives were fantastic. To me they were just ordinary knives. But my dad says the customer is always right.

"I'll sell them to you," I said.

"Sell them to us? Ha! ha! ha!"

All the old babies started to laugh. I had never heard anyone laugh like that before.

"We're not going to buy those knives from you, pipsqueak. We're just going to borrow them."

"What do you mean, borrow them?"

"It means—ha!ha!ha!—that we want them and we're taking them, see, because we need them.

Understand? Ha! ha! ha!"

They all started laughing again and each one picked up a knife.

Well, I was beginning to think that the customer was not always right. A voice inside me was protesting: "That's not borrowing. That's stealing!"

The new neighbour seemed to agree with me, because she jumped up and started to run away, shouting "Help! Thieves!"

Then everything happened very fast.

One of the thieves grabbed my neighbour.

"Stay here, brat, or I'll bash your face."

Then they knocked my table over. They smashed everything and ate up all the cakes. One of the horrible guys stabbed my

doll in the stomach. It cried out
"Mama!"

My neighbour and I threw
ourselves into each other's
arms and stood there together
trembling.

At the end of the block I could see an old lady running away. And even farther away, two little black dots.

Then I got a real shock!

Alexander was there, hiding behind a tree! Then he started crawling across the lawn, like when he's playing war.

He made it to the porch steps, then sprang up and dashed into the house. Whew! The thieves didn't see him. They were having too much fun.

A few seconds later, Julian ran out of the house, with my dad behind him.

"Come back here, Julian!"

It was too late. Julian strode forward with his sword.

"STOP OR I WILL ARREST YOU IN THE NAME OF THE

LAW!"

He got another punch in the nose for his trouble and he lost his new glasses.

My dad came up but he didn't have time to start fighting, because we heard a police siren approaching.

The thieves stopped laughing and began to run. Faster than you could believe, they turned back into little black dots.

WHEW! They were gone. But I didn't feel any better. I felt dizzy. I guess my neighbour did too, because we both went out like lights.

8
That was close!

The police came to our house. They thanked Alexander for calling and congratulated him on his courage. Thanks to him, the Bald Eagle gang had been caught.

Julian asked why the police said that Alexander was such a tremendous zero. My dad had to explain.

"Not zero, Julian, *hero*. A tremendous hero. Because Alexander scared the Bald Eagles away."

Julian took off his broken glasses and lit into the police. "It was me, you joking jackanapes! I sent them scurrying with my invincible sword! Fie upon you, saucy varlets!"

The police officers shrank back and turned red. Then Angelbaby put in her two cents' worth.

" 'Matos!"

I told the police officers about the tomato coming down the stairs and our big fight.

When the police left, they were laughing and saying over and over, "What a family! What a family!"

I think my two brothers were fantastic! If it hadn't been for them, the Bald Eagles would probably have scalped my neighbour and me.

I think my neighbour is fantastic too. Now that I know

her, I don't think she is the least bit weird. Her name is Lola and she comes from South America.

Her parents had to leave their country because of General Ricochet and his gang. They sound like they're worse than the Bald Eagles. Lola was selling cakes to make money to send to people fighting against them.

I didn't tell her that I was holding a lawn sale to make money so I could buy a walk-man. Anyway, I don't need a walkman anymore.

I don't have time to listen to music. Every day Lola and I get together and try to think up a plan to help get rid of General Ricochet and his gang. But selling things is too dangerous.

So is borrowing.

It's funny, I had no trouble getting those two ten-dollar bills back into Alexander's piggy bank.

Still, it made me a little

nervous. I was afraid my parents would catch me at it and think that I was a thief. They would have been very disappointed in me. So would Gran. Whew!

Before borrowing any more money, I'll have to think it over very carefully. Who wants to be afraid all the time? That's no way to live.

Look for these First Novels!
Collect the entire series!

Mooch and Me
The Swank Prank
That's Enough, Maddie
Arthur's Dad
Hang On, Mooch
Swank Talk
Maddie in Goal
The Loonies Arrive
Mooch Gets Jealous
Maddie Wants Music
Arthur Throws a Tantrum
Mikey Mite Goes to School

and more to come!

For more information about these and other fine books for young readers contact

Formac Publishing Company Limited
5502 Atlantic Street
Halifax Nova Scotia B3H 1G4
(902) 421-7022 fax (902) 425-0166